Dear Parents and Educators,

Welcome to Penguin Young Readers! As parents and educators, you know that each child develops at his or her own pace—in terms of speech, critical thinking, and, of course, reading. Penguin Young Readers recognizes this fact. As a result, each Penguin Young Readers book is assigned a traditional easy-to-read level (1–4) as well as a Guided Reading Level (A–P). Both of these systems will help you choose the right book for your child. Please refer to the back of each book for specific leveling information. Penguin Young Readers features esteemed authors and illustrators, stories about favorite characters, fascinating nonfiction, and more!

Benny the Big Shot Goes to Camp

LEVEL 3

GUIDED READING LEVEL **J**

This book is perfect for a **Transitional Reader** who:
• can read multisyllable and compound words;
• can read words with prefixes and suffixes;
• is able to identify story elements (beginning, middle, end, plot, setting, characters, problem, solution); and
• can understand different points of view.

Here are some **activities** you can do during and after reading this book:
• Character Traits: Come up with a list of words to describe Benny. How does his character change at the end of the story?
• Make Predictions: When Benny gets back to camp after the overnight trip, how do you think he will act? Pretend you are Benny and act out a scene. Will Benny still be a big shot? If not, how will he interact with his fellow campers?

Remember, sharing the love of reading with a child is the best gift you can give!

—Bonnie Bader, EdM
  Penguin Young Readers program

*Penguin Young Readers are leveled by independent reviewers applying the standards developed by Irene Fountas and Gay Su Pinnell in *Matching Books to Readers: Using Leveled Books in Guided Reading*, Heinemann, 1999.

To Lauren:
The *best* camper ever—*really*—BB

For Michael, Alexandra, Maxi,
and my new friend, Benny—SW

Penguin Young Readers
Published by the Penguin Group
Penguin Group (USA) Inc., 375 Hudson Street, New York, New York 10014, USA
Penguin Group (Canada), 90 Eglinton Avenue East, Suite 700, Toronto, Ontario M4P 2Y3, Canada
(a division of Pearson Penguin Canada Inc.)
Penguin Books Ltd., 80 Strand, London WC2R 0RL, England
Penguin Group Ireland, 25 St. Stephen's Green, Dublin 2, Ireland (a division of Penguin Books Ltd.)
Penguin Group (Australia), 250 Camberwell Road, Camberwell, Victoria 3124, Australia
(a division of Pearson Australia Group Pty. Ltd.)
Penguin Books India Pvt. Ltd., 11 Community Centre, Panchsheel Park, New Delhi—110 017, India
Penguin Group (NZ), 67 Apollo Drive, Rosedale, Auckland 0632, New Zealand
(a division of Pearson New Zealand Ltd.)
Penguin Books (South Africa) (Pty.) Ltd., 24 Sturdee Avenue,
Rosebank, Johannesburg 2196, South Africa

Penguin Books Ltd., Registered Offices: 80 Strand, London WC2R 0RL, England

Text copyright © 2003 by Bonnie Bader. Illustrations copyright © 2003 by Shari Warren. All rights
reserved. First published in 2003 by Grosset & Dunlap, an imprint of Penguin Group (USA) Inc.
Published in 2012 by Penguin Young Readers, an imprint of Penguin Group (USA) Inc.,
345 Hudson Street, New York, New York 10014. Manufactured in China.

Library of Congress Control Number: 2002151240

ISBN 978-0-448-42894-9   10 9 8 7 6 5 4 3 2 1

Benny the Big Shot Goes to Camp

by Bonnie Bader
illustrated by Shari Warren

Penguin Young Readers
An Imprint of Penguin Group (USA) Inc.

Benny was going to sleepaway camp
for the very first time.

"It's time to pack your bags,"
Benny's mom said.

"Oh, I can do it myself," Benny said.

"I've read the camp list a billion times.

I know just what
I have to bring!"

Benny packed shorts and T-shirts
for warm days.

He packed long pants and
long-sleeved shirts for cool days.

He packed sneakers for running.

He packed hiking boots for hiking.

He packed swimming trunks
for swimming.

He packed a sweater and a sweatshirt.

And he packed lots of socks.

"There," Benny said.

He sat on his trunk.

"I'm done!"

"I think you forgot something,"
Mom said.

"I didn't forget," Benny said.

He grabbed the underwear from
his mom.

"I was just saving them for last!"

Benny's little sister, Mollie,

walked into the room.

"Aren't you scared to go to camp?"

Mollie asked Benny.

"Me? Scared?" Benny said

with a laugh.

"I'm not scared of anything!

I'll be the best camper

Camp Treetop has ever seen!"

"Can I have Benny's room
while he's gone?" Mollie asked.
Mom shook her head.
"Your brother's only going to be
gone for two weeks.
He'll be back before you know it!"

As soon as Mollie and Mom left
the room, Benny put a few more
things into his trunk.

Things that weren't on the camp list.

On Monday morning, Benny left
for camp.

"Good-bye, dear," his mom said.

"Don't get homesick!" Mollie said.

"Don't worry about me!" Benny said.

"I'm going to be the best camper
Camp Treetop has ever seen!"

Benny walked on the bus.

He had a big smile on his face.

None of the other kids were smiling.

A few of the kids were crying.

"What's wrong with you guys?"

Benny asked.

"Sleepaway camp is the best!"

Benny sat down at the back of the bus.

He waved to Mollie.

He blew a kiss to his parents.

And when he was sure

they were out of sight,

he wiped a tear from his cheek.

Finally, the bus reached the camp.

"I'm your counselor, Matt,"
a young man said.

"Welcome to Bunk Three.
Everyone can pick a bunk bed."

"I call bottom," a camper named
Sam said.

"There's no way I can have a top,"
a boy named Tim said.

"I'm afraid of heights."

"What's wrong with you guys?"

Benny asked.

"I *love* the top bunk.

I *always* sleep on the top.

I'm not afraid of heights!"

Benny put down his duffel bag.

He scrambled up the ladder

and plopped on the bed.

"See?" Benny said to the other campers.

"It's great up here!

I'm the king of the hill . . ."

Benny landed on the floor

with a big thump!

Benny looked up at the other campers.

They just stared at him.

Then Benny started to laugh.

"Wasn't that a cool trick?" he said.

Matt helped Benny up.

"Come on, guys," Matt said.

"It's time to go sailing."

"Sailing?" Benny said.

"I love to sail.

I bet I'm the best sailor

Camp Treetop has ever seen!"

They walked down to the lake.

They put on life vests.

"Who wants to go first?" Matt asked.

Benny raised his hand.

Benny and Matt climbed into
the sailboat.

"I know just what to do," Benny
told Matt.

He grabbed a rope.

He grabbed a sail.

And the boat tipped over!

Benny floated to the top of the lake.

Matt grabbed on to him.

"You shouldn't have done that,"

Matt said.

"But I wanted to get wet," Benny said.

"It's very hot out here."

"Let's get back to shore," Matt said.

"It's almost time for woodshop."

"Woodshop?" Benny said.

"I love woodshop.

I bet I'm the best woodworker

Camp Treetop has ever seen!"

"Welcome to woodshop.

I'm Jane.

We're going to build

birdhouses today," Jane said.

Jane gave out the supplies.

"Be careful with the glue," Jane said.

"It's very sticky."

"I'm great with glue," Benny said.

"Be careful with the hammers,"
Jane said.

"They're very heavy."

"I'm very handy with hammers,"
Benny said.

"Is everyone done?" Jane asked.

"Yes!" said the campers.

"Very nice," Jane said as she walked around.

"Oh dear!" Jane cried.

She ran over to Benny.

Benny's birdhouse was stuck
to his hand!

"But I wanted it this way," Benny said.
"This way, I can be very close to the
birds when they come to my birdhouse
to eat."

Luckily, the glue hadn't dried yet.

Over the next few days,

the campers did lots of fun things.

And of course,

Benny said he was the best at all of them.

Benny said he was the best
at baseball.

But he struck out every time.

Benny said he was the best at tennis.

But he lost all the tennis balls.

Benny said he was the best
at gymnastics.
But he kept falling off the
balance beam.

Benny said he was the best at
rock climbing.
But all he did was dangle in the air.

One night, after Benny had fallen
asleep, the campers started to talk.
"I'm tired of Benny's bragging,"
Tim said.
"He thinks he's such a big shot,"
said Sam.
"I think we should teach him a lesson,"
David whispered.
The boys had a plan.

When Benny went outside

the next morning,

he saw all the campers laughing.

They were pointing at the flagpole.

Benny looked up.

There was a blankie dangling

from the pole.

Benny's blankie!

"Okay, big shot," someone called.

"See if you can get your *blankie* down!"

Benny tried to climb up the flagpole.

But each time he tried,

he just slid back down.

Finally, Matt came out to help.

Benny did not brag the rest of the day.

He did not brag the rest of the night.

When it was time for their overnight
camping trip, Benny just packed his
bag and followed along.

The campers went up a steep hill.

And down an even steeper one.

They went across a stream.

And they went under some rocks.

"I'm tired," Tim said.

"Me too," David added.

"Are we there yet?" Sam wanted to know.

Matt stopped walking.

He looked up at the sky.

It was getting dark.

"I'm afraid we're lost," Matt said.

"Lost?" the campers cried.

"I can help," Benny said.

"I can find our way back."

"Yeah, right!"

the campers said.

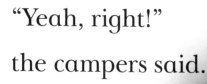

Benny sat down on a rock.

"I know I've said I'm good

at a lot of things," he said.

"And I know the truth is that

I'm not the best at everything.

But I know how to get us

back to camp.

I really do!" he said.

No one believed him.

"I know east from west.

And north from south," Benny said.

"I know which direction to go in

to get us back to camp.

And if you don't believe me,

I'll go myself!"

Benny set off on his own.

It was getting very dark.

"Wait up!" cried Matt.

"Don't leave us," said David.

They all followed Benny.

Under some rocks.

Across a stream.

Up a big hill.

And down a big hill.

"Look!" shouted Tim.

"I see our camp."

"Hooray!" the campers shouted.

"Let's hear it for Benny!" said Matt.

"He's really the best camper

Camp Treetop has ever seen!"